The Sleepover Club

Have you been invited to all these sleepovers?

The S~~leepover~~ Club
at ~~Laura's~~ Kenny's!

MEET MY SISTER,
MOLLY THE MONSTER

by Rose Impey

HarperCollins *Children's Books*

The Sleepover Club ® is a
registered trademark of HarperCollins*Publishers* Ltd

First published as *The Sleepover Club at Kenny's*
in Great Britain by Collins in 1997
This edition published in Great Britain by Collins in 2003

HarperCollins *Children's Books* is a division of HarperCollins*Publishers* Ltd
77-85 Fulham Palace Road, Hammersmith,
London, W6 8JB

The HarperCollins *Children's Books* website address is
www.harpercollinschildrensbooks.co.uk

3 5 7 9 8 6 4 2

Text copyright © Rose Impey 1997

ISBN 0 00 716936 1

The author asserts the moral right to
be identified as the author of this work.

Printed and bound in England by
Clays Ltd, St Ives plc

You are invited to Kenny's
for a sleepover

on Saturday 21 December

My address is
6 Brookside Close
Brook Street
Cuddington
Leicester

Please come at 4pm
and be ready to have
lots of fun!

Love from,

Kenny

Sleepover kit list

1. Sleeping bag
2. Pillow
3. Pyjamas
4. Slippers
5. Toothbrush, toothpaste, soap etc
6. Towel
7. Teddy
8. A creepy story
9. Yummy food for a midnight feast - you know what we're cooking!
10. Torch
11. Hairbrush
12. Hair things, like a bobble or hairband, if you need them
13. Clean knickers and socks
14. Sleepover diary and membership card

CHAPTER ONE

Shall I tell you what I got for Christmas? A pair of shoes with heels. Coo-el. At first my mum said I wasn't old enough for heels.

"I'm ten," I told her. "How old do you have to be?"

Dad said, "You're tall enough already." But he's just worried that one day I'm going to be taller than him.

I really, really wanted them, you know what I mean? So I just kept on and on and in the end... I won! One-nil to me. Yeah!

They've got silver buckles on them. They are drop-dead *gorgeous*. I told Mum and Dad, "You're the best, most groovy parents in the whole wide world." So it was really important to come up with something brill for them.

My dad was easy, I always buy him a big bar of Toblerone. It's his fave chocolate. Then I found the perfect present for Mum: this fat little pig lying down in the mud with all her babies round her. It was so cute. My mum adores pigs, she's got a whole collection. The only trouble was it cost four pounds fifty!

I'm always broke, are you? Kenny is too, money goes through her fingers like water. So we came up with this brilliant idea to earn some, and we got the rest of the Sleepover Club to help us. It was a great plan and we could have been seriously rich, if Kenny's horrible sister, Molly The Monster, hadn't spoiled everything. But don't worry, we got our own back. When we had our last sleepover at Kenny's house we gave her a real scare. It was excellent.

I know, I know, we got grounded again, but listen, it was worth it. She nearly went haywire. And I had the best part in it.

Come on. Let's go up to my room and I'll tell you all about it. But remember, this is Sleepover Club business, so don't tell the others I told you.

Can you remember everyone? Laura McKenzie, otherwise known as Kenny. Fliss – her real name – Felicity Sidebotham. Lyndsey Collins – we call her Lyndz, we've been friends since we first started school. And Rosie Cartwright. And me, of course: Francesca Theresa Thomas, but everyone calls me Frankie.

Now where should I start?

I suppose it really started early in December, the day we were helping our teacher, Mrs Weaver, put up the Christmas decorations in the hall. It was a great skive, it took all afternoon. She kept having to go out to check on the rest of the class so we spent most of the time wrapping ourselves up in paper chains and Chinese lanterns. It was such a laugh. Then we started talking about Christmas presents and what we were going to buy each other. After that I didn't feel like laughing.

"I've got all your presents and they're already wrapped," said Fliss.

I couldn't believe it.

"What've you got us?" said Kenny, straight out, just like that.

"The new Oasis tape." Fliss looked so pleased with herself.

"What, all of us?" said Rosie. "Wowsers!"

The others were dead excited but at first all I could think was: *it's just not fair*. Fliss has so much more money than the rest of us. She gets loads of pocket money. Even Lyndz can earn extra by helping her mum with Spike, their baby, but Rosie and

Kenny and me just get regular pocket money and it's never enough, especially at Christmas. Fliss had spent nearly as much money on each of us as I had to spend on everyone put together.

When I went home I tried to talk to my mum and dad about it but it was a waste of time. My mum and dad are lawyers; they have an answer for everything.

"Please, can I have some extra money? I really need it. Fliss has spent pounds on my Christmas present."

"How do you know that?" said Dad. "Did she leave the price on?"

"Of course not. But everyone knows what tapes cost."

"Well, perhaps Felicity can afford to spend that much on her friends, but it's no reason why you need to," said Mum.

"Remember it's Christmas," said Dad. "It's not a competition."

Well, I knew that. My grandma's always telling me, it's not the gift that counts, it's the thought behind it. But it wasn't just Fliss's present I was worried about. I needed money for everyone's. I went upstairs and emptied my purse and counted my money. But I'd only counted it half an hour earlier and it still only came to £8.43. If I spent £4.50 on my mum's pig I'd have less than £4 to spend on everyone else put together. I wrote a list of the people I wanted to give presents to: Mum & Dad, Grandma, Grandad, Kenny, Fliss, Lyndz, Rosie and some chews for Pepsi, my dog. It just wasn't enough and you didn't have to be Mastermind to work that out.

I needed a good moan, so I got on the phone to Kenny. She's my best friend after all and that's what best friends are for.

"Hiya. It's me, Frankie."

"Oh, hi, Frankie."

"I am so broke. I've only got £8.43 in all the world."

"Well, that's more than I've got."

"I don't know how I can possibly be expected to get all my Christmas presents with a measly £8.43."

"No, nor me."

"And now Fliss has spent pounds on us I feel terrible only spending 50p on her."

"Mmmm. Me too."

This conversation was not helping at all. It was a bit like talking into a black hole. What we needed here was some action.

I said, "So! What are we going to do?"

"Rob a bank?"

"Oh, Kenny, be serious. We need to find some way of making money where we won't end up in jail."

"OK. Let's both make a list. I'll ring you back."

I sat down with a pen and a pad and tried to come up with some ideas, but the more I thought about it the madder I got. There are a few things about my family which I don't think are at all fair. For example, I am an only child, which I think

15

is completely unfair. I keep telling my parents how much I'd like a brother or sister, but they don't take any notice. Although, come to think of it, if I had, it would mean an extra present to buy!

Another thing is that I already do all sorts of jobs which other people could get extra pocket money for, like walking the dog for instance. Yes, I know she's my dog, but even so… And like washing up, or drying and putting away. Other people get extra money for doing that, but I'm expected to do it anyway. Mum and Dad are always telling me, "We're a team, Frankie. We all do our share. That's fair, isn't it?"

I suppose it is, but it doesn't help me make any money, does it? The other thing is, my mum and dad don't give me as much pocket money as other people get, even though they could afford to, because they don't believe in *spoiling* me! Huh! I wish. They think all the adverts on TV make children want lots of things they don't really need, and I suppose they do. But this is different. This is to buy presents for other people, for them even.

But they have an answer to that too. My mum and dad would be happy if I just made them something out of egg boxes, because, yeah, yeah, I know – it's the thought that counts. I just wish all my friends knew that!

At least Kenny did. And, however broke I was, I knew that Kenny was more broke. She's a disaster area where money's concerned.

CHAPTER TWO

Kenny can't earn extra pocket money washing up or drying the pots either, because they've got a dishwasher. She used to be able to earn a bit extra if she loaded it for her mum, but not any more. Last summer they had this big birthday barbecue and Kenny loaded it with paper plates which disintegrated and blocked up the outlet and they had to call a plumber.

"How was I to know?" she said. "They were dead cute plates, with shells and fish on. I thought you'd want to use them again."

"Not much chance of that, now they're sandblasted onto the sides of the dishwasher," her dad yelled at her.

Anyway since then she hasn't been allowed to do any jobs in the kitchen.

Helping out in the garden was another idea, but there's not much to do in December. And Kenny's dad said he had no intention of spring cleaning their garage at this time of year just to please us. So that was that. Back to the drawing board, as my dad says.

"What about washing cars?" Kenny suggested at last.

"That's the first sensible idea you've had," I said. "Whose shall we start on?"

We started on my mum's VW and we were just in the middle of doing it when Lyndz came round on her mountain bike. We're usually dead pleased to see Lyndz but this time we weren't, for obvious reasons.

"Hiya. What're you doing?" she said.

"Crocheting a pair of mittens for the dog!" I said. "What does it look like?"

Lyndz grinned. "Can I help?"

Kenny and I looked down at our feet and sighed. We were both hoping she wouldn't ask that. My mum had agreed to pay Kenny and me 50p each, if we did a good job and didn't leave too much mess. We'd been really sensible and we'd nearly finished, so we didn't want to have to share it with Lyndz. But we both felt really mean leaving her out.

"OK," I said. "But no water fights, or else." I don't know why I even bothered saying that. When Kenny and Lyndz get together they always go bananas. Like that time they had a shopping trolley race in the supermarket and knocked down a humungous stack of bottles of mineral water.

Fortunately, this time Mum didn't go too mad because it was only soapy water they were throwing around and they got most of it over themselves. In fact she gave us all 50p *and* an ice lolly each.

After that we all cycled round to Kenny's house and persuaded her mum to let us clean her Fiesta. And then Kenny's next-door neighbour, Bert, who's really nice, said we could do his. We didn't charge him as much because he's a pensioner. But by the end of the afternoon we'd each made £1.25.

"This is great," said Kenny. "We'll soon be rich."

"How do you make that out?" I said. "My mum won't have her car cleaned again for months." And I knew my dad wouldn't let us loose on his BMW, he's too proud of it.

"We'll ask the other neighbours," she said. "Down your road and in our close."

"What? You mean knock on people's doors?"

"We'll put a note through their letter boxes, like a proper business."

"Are you mad?" I said.

"I think it's a great idea," said Lyndz. So that was it. I was outvoted, which was a bit off since I was the one who'd started it all. But that was only the beginning. On Monday morning, when old Bossyboots Fliss heard about it, she took over straight away.

"Listen, I've got a great idea: we can print the notices out on Frankie's computer," she said, "so we look really professional."

"We?" I said. "Since when did you need to earn any money? You're loaded already."

"Well, I'm not," said Rosie. "I could do with earning some money before Christmas. Adam wants a new game for his computer and I said I'd give Tiff something towards it." Adam is Rosie's brother, he's computer-mad. And Tiff is Rosie's older sister. She's fifteen and she works after school in the local supermarket, so she could afford it on her own really.

"Listen," said Kenny. "If we do it together and get properly organised, we'll be much quicker, so we'll do more cars, so we'll earn more money, so there'll be enough for all of us."

"Yeah," said Lyndz. "And it'll be more fun, if it's all five of us."

I nodded. I supposed she was right. But I had a funny feeling that things were already getting out of hand. It felt like another of those times when, as my gran says, it would all end in tears.

After school everyone came round to my house and we went up to my bedroom. I'm not supposed to have friends round after school, I'm supposed to go next door to Auntie Joan's until my mum and dad get home from work, and watch TV with the gruesome Nathan. He's not my cousin, thank goodness. And Joan's not my real auntie, I just call her that. But she's a good sport and she said that just this once we could go up and play on my computer, and she'd look in on us and bring us some cookies, when they came out of the oven.

"You're the best," I said and gave her a hug.

"Make sure you're sensible," she warned us and she gave me our front door key.

We threw our coats on my bed and I turned on my computer.

"OK. What shall we call ourselves?" said Fliss.

"Call ourselves?"

"Yeah. You need a catchy name, so people remember it."

"What about, *Sleepover Club Car Wash*," said Lyndz.

"That's no good," said Kenny. "It sounds as if we'll be going to sleep on the job."

"I know," said Fliss, "A1 Car Cleaners. That way we'll get to be first in the phone book. Andy told me lots of businesses do that." Andy is sort of Fliss's step-dad and he's a plumber so I suppose he should know.

"Get a life," I said. "We're never going to get in the phone book."

"We've got to think big," said Kenny. But even she could see that was a *stoopid* idea.

In the end, we called ourselves: Five Star Car Wash which was much better, because there are five of us and five star means the best. You can probably guess whose idea that was! No, it wasn't Fliss's, actually. It was mine, thank you very much.

This is what our notice looked like:

★ ★ ★ ★ ★

Five Star Car Wash

On your own doorstep!
We'll bring our own bucket and sponge

**ONLY £1.50 PER CAR.
FRANKIE THOMAS:
17 THE RIDGEWAY !**

At first we couldn't agree how much we should charge. We finally settled on £1.50, which seemed a lot, but we had to share it between five. Still, as Kenny had said, we'd be able to clean more cars so we'd earn more in the long run.

Then we printed off half the notices for Kenny's close, with her name and address on the bottom and the other half for my road with my name on the bottom.

"We can start on Fliss's street later," I said.

"If we're not too busy," said Kenny.

We were really excited. Before they left, everyone helped me post the notices through all the doors in my road. We rushed to get them done, before my mum and dad came home.

I know! You needn't look like that. I wasn't going to keep it a secret forever; I did intend telling them. I just thought I'd wait for the right moment... when they were both in a good mood... tomorrow, perhaps… or the next day.

And it wasn't easy, not to tell them, because that night I was nearly bursting to. I lay in bed planning all the things I'd buy when I was rich. And I probably would have been, if Molly the Monster hadn't stuck her nose in where it didn't belong.

CHAPTER THREE

Have I told you before about Kenny's sister Molly? She's gruesome. Poor old Kenny has to share a bedroom with her and she hates it. It's not a very big room and there are two beds in it with a dressing table between them. There isn't even room for a wardrobe, that's out on the landing. Molly is so bossy she's always making rules about what Kenny can and can't do in her own bedroom.

For example, Kenny has a pet rat, called Merlin. He has to live in the garage. Molly won't allow her to have him in the bedroom. Kenny has to go outside if she wants to play with him.

The other thing she does is to draw a line with chalk down the middle of the dressing table and if anything of Kenny's slides over onto her side she throws it away! I mean it. That's really hard for Kenny, because she's a bit untidy at the best of times. She's always finding her things chucked in the waste basket. All Molly says is, "Well, you'd better keep them on your own side, then, hadn't you?" Honestly!

Kenny and Molly have always fallen out, ever since Kenny was little. She's almost lost count of the horrible things Molly has done. Once, when they were on holiday, she pushed Kenny out of bed and nearly broke her arm. And another time, when Kenny was really small, Molly cut off her hair, all of it, except a little sprout which stuck out at the front. Kenny's still got a photo of it. She looks like a Cabbage Patch doll.

And then the worst time was when their dad was digging a pond in the garden; while he was mixing the cement to lay the base, Molly buried all Kenny's Playpeople in the hole. She only told her after the pond was finished and filled with water and it had fish in it. That's what she's like, gruesome with a capital GRRR!

Molly hates it when we have a sleepover at their house, because she has to move out and sleep on the camp bed in Emma's room. Emma is their other sister, she's sixteen, which is the reason she has a room to herself while Kenny and Molly have to share. So, whenever we sleepover at Kenny's, we can't get rid of Molly. She hangs around, telling us all the things we're not allowed to do, like touching her jewellery, as if we'd want to, or getting on her bed with our shoes on, as if we would, and *looking at* her make-up.

"How does looking at it wear it out?" I said.

Kenny pulled a being sick face. "*She* certainly needs make-up," she said. "She could do with a complete mask."

"I heard that," said Molly. She was hiding behind the door. That's the other thing, she's always ear-wigging on our conversations and it really gets on our nerves.

But sometimes Kenny gets her own back. Molly's twelve and she's got one or two tiny spots starting. She peers at them in the mirror so Kenny tells her how they're getting bigger and one day they'll cover her whole face. Last time we were there we made this mixture of salt and pepper in water and told her it was a secret recipe Lyndz's grandma had given her for spot lotion and we'd made it specially for her.

"I haven't got spots," she shrieked. "I

have not got spots!" She nearly went ballistic!

We hadn't had a sleepover at Kenny's for ages, because of Molly. Poor old Kenny's tried complaining to her mum and dad but they always say the same thing. Kenny knows it off by heart: "We've only got three bedrooms. Emma's the oldest; she's got GCSEs this year; she needs a room of her own to study in. Anyway, we both shared bedrooms with our brothers and sisters when we were your age. It's good for you to share."

"Good for me?" Kenny screamed at us. "How can it be good for me? I'll be lucky if I live to be twelve. I'd rather sleep out in the garage with Merlin."

"Why don't your family move?" said Rosie. "Get a bigger house."

"We've been trying to for ages, but we can't find one Mum likes. Dad doesn't care; he's never there." Kenny's dad's a doctor, he works all the time. "But Mum is so fussy.

The house has got to be exactly what she wants and it never is."

Kenny was telling us about it while we were waiting for netball practice. She was even more steamed up than usual with Molly because that morning she'd found her *Girl Talk* comic screwed up in the waste basket and she'd only read half of it.

"How was I to know?" said Molly. "It was on the floor. You should put your things away."

"I'd flatten her," I said.

"*You* probably could," said Kenny. "But she's bigger than me."

"Why don't you tell your mum and dad?" asked Fliss.

"I already did, but what's the point? They don't do anything."

"I thought you had a caravan," said Rosie. "Why not ask if you can sleep in that?"

Everyone went quiet and looked at their feet. "It's haunted," said Kenny.

"Haunted?"

Kenny nodded. "Poltergeist."

Rosie's eyes nearly popped out of her head, but Kenny didn't want to get started on that story. None of us like that story, it's too creepy. So we got back to the important subject.

"Anyway," said Kenny, "it's my turn for you all to sleepover at my house next, so we need to start thinking of some juicy revenges for Monster-face. Anybody got any good ideas?"

Ideas? We had loads. It was pay back time for Molly The Monster and we were really looking forward to it.

CHAPTER FOUR

But before I tell you about that, let's get back to the car wash business, which was not going too well. Before we even had a chance to get started my mum and dad found out what we were up to and they were not pleased. It was Auntie Joan's fault.

On Tuesday and Wednesday, when I got in from school, I kept waiting for our first customer to ring or knock on the door. Kenny was phoning every five minutes to check whether I'd heard anything, because she still hadn't, so I had to tell her to get off the phone in case anyone was trying to ring us. But there was nothing. Not a sausage.

Then, on Wednesday night, Mum and Dad saw the notice. They were having a cup of coffee in Auntie Joan's kitchen and they saw it stuck on her notice board.

"*Five Star Car Wash*! What's all that about?"

"Frankie!"

Thank goodness they didn't go *too* mad. They just had a medium-sized wobbly. But they said I should have told them first; then they could have saved me the trouble of doing the notices. Which they said were very good. But, grrrrr, they still wouldn't let me do it. And shall I tell you why? Because I wasn't *old enough*. I'm never old enough for anything, according to them.

"The law's quite clear about it," said Dad. "Children under thirteen are not allowed to do paid work, so that's that."

"But all my friends do," I said. "*Other people* get extra pocket money for picking the newspaper up off the floor."

"Pocket money's different," said Mum. "Parents can give as much or as little pocket money as they like. We're talking about people outside the family paying children to work. It's against the law."

"But it's only car washing," I said. "Everybody does it."

"Not lawyers' daughters," said Mum.

"Especially this lawyer's daughter," said Dad. "Case closed. No room for appeal."

So, I was right, wasn't I? I knew if I told them, they'd say no. I guess that's why Kenny didn't tell her mum and dad either. But they still found out – thanks to Molly.

Monster-face is in the same class at school as Howard Jinks. He's a boy who lives down their road. He's gross. He's always thumping people. He took one of our notices into school and showed it to people in their class. Then everyone started calling Molly 'Five Star Car Wash' all day, and asking her where her bucket and sponge were. When she came home she was fizzing like an unexploded bomb.

She stuffed the note in Kenny's face. "If this is your idea of a joke, it isn't funny."

"It wasn't meant to be funny. We were trying to earn some money, that's all."

"Well, you can forget it," said Molly. "You're in big trouble." And she rushed into the kitchen, yelling her head off, to find their mum.

Kenny's mum was cross because she was in the middle of cutting someone's hair at the time. Kenny's mum does some hairdressing at home and she said Molly had shown her up in front of the lady. So she got a good telling off, hah! But later, when their dad came home and saw the notice, they both gave Kenny a *serious talking to*.

They said she definitely should have asked their permission; which Kenny knew. They said she certainly shouldn't have been wandering up and down the street, knocking on people's doors, because it wasn't safe to do that nowadays. Kenny told them we hadn't knocked on any doors, we'd just posted our notices through the letter boxes. And they said, she wasn't anything like old enough (yawn, yawn) to be washing other people's cars, it was too much responsibility. If she did any damage they'd have to pay the bill. Kenny tried to point out that you can't do much damage with a sponge and a plastic bucket, but they said that wasn't the point.

But the good news was they didn't actually say she couldn't do it! They said *if* anyone answered the advert and, *if* it was someone they knew, they'd think about it.

That was when Molly the Bomb exploded. "Is that it!" she yelled. "Is she going to get away with this? Are you going to let her off as easy as that? I don't believe this!"

"It's nothing to do with you," said Kenny. "Mind your own business."

"This is my business. If you go showing me up at school, it's my business."

"Oh, go and boil your head," said Kenny.

But after that Molly was even more horrible to her and did everything she could to get Kenny into trouble and instead of just having a chalk line down the middle of the dressing table, she used a piece of rope to divide the room up and said Kenny couldn't even step in her half of the room which is stupid because Molly's got the door in her half.

"I'm sick of you," Kenny told her.

"So what are you going to do about it?" said Molly, lounging on her bed.

"I'm going to fix you. You just wait."

"Oh, yeah. You and whose army?"

"Me and my Sleepover Club army," thought Kenny. But she didn't say anything. She thought she'd keep that as a surprise.

"I hate my sister," she told us the next morning on the way to school. "I'm going to sue her. Frankie, will you ask your mum and dad how I do it?"

"I don't think you can sue your sister just for being gruesome," I told her.

"Well, you ought to be able to. She's going to be a criminal when she grows up and I'm sick of her practising on me."

"So what are you going to do?" said Rosie.

"I don't know. Yet."

"Have you asked your mum and dad about the sleepover?" said Fliss.

Kenny sighed again. "They said it's too close to Christmas, but I'm not giving up."

Have you noticed how unfair it is around Christmas? I don't know about your parents, but mine are always going out to parties with their friends, eating vol-au-vents and sausage rolls and having a great time, but the minute I ask to have a party, or have my friends round, they go on about how busy they are. And Kenny's parents are just the same.

There was only one weekend left before

Christmas. We couldn't bear to wait until after the holidays. Kenny begged her mum and dad on bended knees, pretty please, the whole works. No luck. So then she promised them all sorts of things, if they'd let her: she'd tidy her bedroom, stop biting her nails, even eat cabbage. When that didn't work either, she threatened to run away. The trouble is Kenny's done that loads of times. When she was little, every time she fell out with Molly, she used to write a note for her mum to say she was running away, then she'd just sneak upstairs and hide under her bed. So now her mum knows exactly where to find her.

In the end Kenny was so desperate she did a really big thing. She told us it was the *ultimate sacrifice* and she was prepared to make it, for the Sleepover Club. That's the kind of person Kenny is. That's why she's my all-time best friend.

She agreed to wear a dress on Christmas Day. Oh, you may think that's nothing, because I bet you wear dresses or skirts all the time, but it was really big for Kenny. Kenny lives and dies in her Leicester City football strip. Her mum tries everything to get her out of it, for at least one day a year. So she was really pleased. In fact, you'd have thought Kenny had given her a present.

Kenny had to promise in front of the whole family *and* sign a piece of paper. But she did it. The sleepover was settled for Saturday night. And Molly was *furious!*

"You mean to say I've got to give up my bed for those little gonks. It's not fair. I never have friends round to stay."

"That's because you haven't got any friends," said Kenny.

"I have too. Anyway, how come she gets everything she wants? She's so spoiled. I won't do it. I won't! You can't make me."

But they did. Hee-hee-hee-hee-hee! One-nil to Kenny!

CHAPTER FIVE

Kenny couldn't wait for school the next morning. She came rushing to find us with the good news. She was late because she'd been to the dentist with her mum. The rest of us were already in the hall, rehearsing for the Christmas Concert. Well, actually we were waiting for Mrs Weaver to get round to our part, so we were at the back of the hall, supposed to be practising our lines.

"OK," she said. "The sleepover's on Saturday night. So it's PBT for Monster-face."

"PBT?" said Fliss.

"Pay back time for Molly," I said. Sometimes she's so slow.

"Oh, yeah," said Fliss.

"Let's start planning it," said Rosie.

"Someone slip back to the classroom and get a notebook," said Fliss.

I said, "What did your last servant die of?"

"I'll go," said Lyndz. Lyndz likes to keep the peace.

It didn't matter about practising because we all knew our lines back to front and standing on our heads. No, I mean it. We'd been practising handstands at the back of the hall and reciting our lines at the same time, because it was boring, just waiting around. Mrs Weaver didn't seem to mind as long as we kept quiet. She'd been rehearsing Alana Palmer and Regina Hill for over half an hour.

Alana Palmer couldn't remember any of her lines and Regina Hill kept changing hers. Regina Hill's this weird new girl who's just started in our class. She's even taller than me. And she's so stuck up. She's nearly as bad as the M&Ms, our worst enemies. She even argues with the teacher. She was just making her lines up as she went along and they were different every time, so Alana never knew when to come in.

Between them they were driving Mrs Weaver mad, but at least it gave us time to plan our sleepover. Lyndz handed the notebook to me. I always have to do the writing.

"We could make Molly an apple pie bed," said Rosie. "After we've used the bed for the sleepover, of course. Before we go home."

"Won't that make a terrible mess?" said Fliss. "My mum'd have a fit."

"You don't use apple pies, dumbo," I said.

"We just make the bed so Molly can't get into it," said Kenny.

"What for?" said Fliss.

"To annoy her, of course."

Fliss rolled her eyes; she still couldn't see the point.

"Well, you come up with something better, then," I said.

"We could make some fairy cakes with plastic flies in them," said Lyndz suddenly.

"Yeah, great," said Rosie. "But where will we get the flies?"

"Joke shop," said Lyndz. "I've seen them."

"We could use real flies," said Kenny. "And spiders..."

"And slugs," I said. "And worms..."

"And woodlice..."

"Oh, gross," said Rosie.

"Great," said Kenny.

"I don't know," said Fliss. "Flies carry germs. I would have thought you'd have known that, Kenny."

"I do know it. I still think it's a good idea."

"Better stick to plastic," said Rosie.

"What about the spot mixture?" said Lyndz. "That really got her going."

"Yeah, but we've done that. We need something new. Something seriously nasty."

The trouble is we knew the really nasty things we'd like to have done would get us into big trouble. Like the time we drew five moustaches on Molly's poster of the Spice Girls. They looked so funny, we nearly died laughing, but she didn't; she went into orbit. We got a real telling off *and* we had to club together to buy her a new poster.

We needed to think of things where we wouldn't leave any evidence behind us. Things where it would be her word against ours. Even better, things where she wouldn't even know for sure it was us. Hmmm. It needed some thinking about. And we'd only got two days before the sleepover.

We didn't have another chance to work on our list that day because, when we went back to the classroom, Mrs Weaver worked us twice as hard as usual to make up for all the time we'd spent not doing our work when we were in the hall. As if the Christmas Concert was our idea!

At lunchtime, when we might have had time, we got into this argument about when we should give each other our Christmas presents. I hadn't bought mine yet. I was still hoping to earn some more money. I knew I couldn't do any car washing in our road; my mum and dad had put their foot down about that. But if Kenny's mum and dad let her do some in their close I could help. She hadn't heard a thing from any of the neighbours yet, which I thought was a bit strange, but we were still hopeful. So I wanted us to swop presents on the last day of term which would give us nearly a week more.

"But it's our last sleepover before Christmas," said Fliss, whingeing again.

"Well? It doesn't have to be *then*," I said.

"But why not?"

"I haven't bought all your presents yet." The real truth was, I hadn't bought any.

"You can get them on Saturday, before you come."

"Yeah, that's what I'm going to do," said Rosie.

Kenny and I didn't want to admit we hadn't even got the money to get them then.

"I might not have time, anyway," said Kenny. "I shall be busy getting ready." The others all looked at her. "Tidying up and things."

Even I had to laugh. Kenny doesn't know the meaning of tidying up.

"It would be more special," said Rosie, "to swap presents at the sleepover."

"Let's vote on it," said Fliss, bossing again.

Three against two. We were outvoted. So that was how it was left. We just crossed our fingers, hoping that someone in Kenny's close would book a carwash before Saturday.

Kenny did everything she could. All week she'd been smiling and waving to the neighbours, trying to be nice and polite. One or two of them had given her these funny embarrassed smiles and sort of shaken their heads. It was Saturday morning before she found out why. She met Bert's wife coming out of her gate next door.

"You tell your mum and dad they didn't need to send Molly round to apologise, my duck. We thought it was a clever idea of yours, trying to raise some money. We weren't in the least bit offended. It's a shame they won't let you do it."

Kenny couldn't believe her ears. No wonder no one in the close had rung her up. Molly had been round to every house and collected up the notices and told the neighbours that Kenny wasn't allowed to wash their cars and that their mum and dad had sent *her* round to apologise about Kenny being such a nuisance! And, then, as if that wasn't bad enough, the horrible toad had torn our notices up into hundreds of pieces and flushed them down the toilet. When we found out we'd have liked to flush her down the toilet.

Kenny rang to tell me all about it. "Frankie, don't speak. Don't say a word. You're never going to believe this. My sister is unbelievable!"

Afterwards we were both fizzing mad. Now she'd gone too far.

"This means war," said Kenny. "I'll see you later, Frankie."

"Yeah. See you," I said. Which I knew sounded pretty feeble but I couldn't think what else to say. I was still in shock. And when I put down the phone I realised I was still too broke to buy any presents and now my last chance had gone and I'd have to go to the sleepover without any.

CHAPTER SIX

Kenny had told us to arrive for the sleepover at about four o'clock. She'd persuaded her mum to let us come early because we wanted to get started on the *cooking*. You know… the plastic fly cakes! Kenny's mum's really good like that, she often lets us do some cooking. Usually she stays and does it with us, but this time we needed to be on our own.

Kenny had persuaded her we could make fairy cakes with our eyes closed; we'd made them loads of times at school.

So she'd put all the ingredients out on the worktop for us and said we could call out if we needed her. We dumped our bags in Kenny's room and raced down to the kitchen and put aprons on.

The house was full, because everyone was in, even Kenny's dad was at home for once. He was sitting in the lounge watching the football. Emma had a friend round and they were up in the bathroom, dyeing Emma's hair. Kenny's mum was wrapping Christmas presents on the dining-room table and Molly was helping her. So we had the kitchen to ourselves, at least for the moment.

Kenny closed the kitchen door and said, "OK. Let's do this really quickly before anyone comes in. Frankie, you put the paper cases in the tin. Fliss, you whisk these eggs. Lyndz, turn the oven on. Rosie, weigh out the currants."

Rosie started to grin. "The plastic flies, you mean."

We all bit our lips to stop us from giggling. We didn't want Lyndz to start hiccuping because we knew there'd be no stopping her and we needed to get on.

Kenny put all the ingredients in the bowl and beat the mixture so hard it flew up in the air. When her arm started to ache she passed it round and we all had a go. It wasn't a Christmas cake, but we all had a wish anyway. We didn't tell each other what we'd wished for, but we could tell by the soppy grin on Fliss's face what her wish was about. She wants to marry Ryan Scott, who is a really *stoopid* boy in our class. I despair of her sometimes.

Then we all crowded round while Rosie poured the currants in.

"Who's got the *you-know-whats*?" whispered Kenny.

Lyndz took a plastic bag out of her tracksuit pocket. She emptied it out on the worktop. Two plastic spiders fell out.

"They're not flies," hissed Kenny.

"They'd sold out of flies," said Lyndz. "That's all they'd got."

"They're miles too big," yelled Kenny.

"Shhh," I said, terrified her mum would come in. "We'll cut the legs off. Where does your mum keep her scissors?"

Kenny was still giving Lyndz a hard stare, so I went to a drawer and found a pair of scissors. They were pretty big but they would hardly cut butter. I could probably have chewed the legs off quicker. Kenny plopped a dollop of mixture in each of the paper cases and then I pushed the two plastic spiders into the mixture.

"This is never going to work," said Kenny. "They'll probably climb to the top when they're cooking and give the game away."

"They're not climbing anywhere," I said, "with no legs!" But, just in case, I gave the cakes another poke with my finger. Then I scraped round the bowl to get a bit more mixture and heaped the two cake cases higher. Kenny was just about to put the tray in the oven when Rosie said, "Shouldn't we mark them, then we'll know which ones the spiders are in?"

"Good thinking, Batman," I said. "What shall we use?"

"We could put a cherry on those two," said Fliss. "If your mum's got any."

"That's no good," said Kenny. "Molly hates cherries. She'd never eat them."

"That's even better," I said. "We'll put cherries on all the others."

"Mega-brain strikes again," said Kenny, darting into the pantry and coming back with a tub of cherries. She stuck one on each of them, apart from the *special* ones. Thank goodness we'd put them in the oven and disposed of the leftover legs, and started to clear up, before Kenny's dad put his face round the door.

"Mmmm, something smells good. Any chance of a cuppa?" he said.

"Okay," said Kenny. "We'll do it in a minute."

"No hurry. In fact, I'm happy to wait till the cakes are ready."

When they came out of the oven they looked and smelt scrummy. The good news was the spiders hadn't climbed to the top. The bad news was Kenny hadn't pressed the cherries down hard enough and two or three had fallen off. So then we had a bit of an argument about which ones they'd fallen off and whether we could still be sure which were the *special* ones. Luckily, thanks to my idea of putting an extra spoonful of mixture on top, the special cakes were noticeably bigger.

Kenny made a cup of tea for her mum and dad, while I arranged the cakes on a plate. We put Molly's on a small Peter Rabbit plate, and Lyndz poured a glass of orange juice, specially for her, with some salt and pepper in it!

By the time we took them through, Kenny's mum had finished wrapping presents and Molly was sitting on the sofa watching the end of the match with her dad. Kenny gave them their drinks. We all crowded into the lounge and I offered the cake plate to her mum. And then disaster struck.

Before I could offer her dad one, he helped himself to one off Molly's plate.

"You can't eat that," said Kenny, as if it was about to bite him. "It's Molly's," she added quickly. "She doesn't like cherries. We made two without, specially for her. "

"That's OK," Molly said, handing him the plate. "You can have them both. I wouldn't touch them anyway, knowing who made them." And she gave Kenny a horrible look.

"Never mind, peanut," said her dad, winking at Kenny. "All the more for me." And he took the plate and bit into one.

"What the...." but he never finished his sentence because he must have bitten hard into one of the spiders and cracked a filling. He nearly went ballistic.

59

Uh-oh. We really thought we were in for it. We all went so red that we looked like a bad case of sunburn, especially Fliss. But no one noticed. They were all more concerned with Kenny's dad and what he could do about his tooth.

"This is so typical. Why do these things have to happen on a Saturday afternoon? And so close to Christmas. When am I going to get it fixed in the next few days?"

"I don't understand how you can crack a filling on a fairy cake," said her mum.

Fortunately, just then Emma and her friend Hayley raced down to see what had happened and Emma dripped hair dye on the carpet so there was even more fuss about that. And then the football match finished in a draw. Big tragedy! Apparently it was a match Leicester needed to win and Kenny's dad said that was the final straw. He sank back on the sofa, clutching his head. Even Kenny started behaving as if there'd been a national disaster.

I looked at Rosie, who isn't interested in football either, and we rolled our eyes to the ceiling. But then she kept on giving me funny looks until I noticed what she was looking at – the plate with the two cakes. It was still sitting there on the arm of the sofa. While everyone was making a fuss, I picked it up and slipped into the kitchen and tipped them both into the bin.

When I came back Kenny's dad was saying again, "Why do things like this always have to happen when I'm on call?"

"I don't see what difference that makes," said her mum.

"Well, I could have rung Herman. He might have done a quick repair for me. He owes me a favour." Herman was a good friend of Kenny's dad's, as well as being his dentist.

"Oh, Jim, why don't you ring him? It's worth a try."

So, even though it was Saturday teatime, the dentist told him to come right over.

Kenny's dad got his coat on and hunted for his car keys. We were just beginning to relax and think we'd got away with it, when he came back in and said, "I'd like to know what you girls put in those cakes. It felt like biting on a bullet."

Kenny looked as if she might burst, she was so red, but her mum said, "Now, Jim, don't go blaming the girls. There was nothing wrong with my cake; it was delicious. You know what your teeth are like: if there's one seed left in a currant you'll be the one to find it. You've had that filling replaced twice before."

"All the same I might just take it along as evidence," he said, looking round for it.

"Oh, get off with you," said her mum. And lucky for us he did.

It was a good job I'd disposed of the evidence, because Monster-face was watching us all, as if she suspected something was going on. So, to throw her off the scent, we sat down and scoffed the rest of the cakes. "Mmmm, they're so light," I said.

"And soft," agreed Kenny.

"They melt in your mouth," said Rosie.

"Scrummy," said Lyndz. "Sure you don't want the last one?" she asked Molly.

Molly screwed up her nose as an answer. She still hadn't touched her drink either.

"You don't know what you're missing," I said, finishing the last one.

"You'd think we were trying to poison you," said Kenny. And after that we couldn't keep our faces straight. We just raced off upstairs to Kenny's bedroom and collapsed on her bed. But there was no chance to talk about anything, because guess who followed us!

CHAPTER SEVEN

Molly stood in the doorway, glaring at us. "Remember, half of this room is mine and you're not to touch anything."

"Yeah, yeah, you already told us fifty times before," said Kenny and she got up and closed the door on her. For a change Molly didn't open it and start up again.

We were dying to talk about what had happened, but we knew she'd be standing outside ear-wigging. So Kenny got up and put on her cassette player really loud and we huddled together on her bed and whispered.

"That was a lucky escape," I said. "It's a good job Rosie spotted the cakes."

"And you got rid of the evidence," said Rosie.

"I feel really bad about my dad," said Kenny.

Lyndz said, "Yeah, so do I." In fact we all did. None of us liked going to the dentist.

"And we still haven't got our revenge on you-know-who." Kenny pointed to the door.

Somehow making an apple pie bed in the morning seemed a pathetic idea. But later on we came up with a much better one. I'll tell you how it happened.

About half-past six Kenny's mum called us down for tea. She'd made us vegetable lasagne which was *de-licious*. Fortunately Molly the Monster didn't eat with us, because she'd taken herself off to bed. She *said* she felt ill. Well, she couldn't blame it on our cakes because she hadn't touched them or her orange juice. She didn't really look ill. Kenny said it was just an excuse to have their mum running up and down-stairs after her.

Emma and her friend Hayley were going to cook for themselves later on. They were making chicken masala, which I didn't fancy in the least, but then I'm a vegetarian, but the afters, hot fudge bananas, looked scrummy. They said they *might* save us some, if we kept out of their way.

While we were still eating there was a phone call from Kenny's dad to say he'd got his tooth fixed and he was going to stay a bit longer and have a cup of coffee with Herman. Then about half an hour later there was another call to say he'd been bleeped so he was going on now to see a patient and he'd be home later.

After we'd finished eating we carried the dishes through to the kitchen. Kenny's mum loaded them into the dishwasher and then sent us through to the lounge because Emma and Hayley were already starting their cooking and it isn't a very big kitchen.

Over the back of a chair in the lounge was one of the hairdressing gowns Kenny's mum uses, so I just threw it over my head and crept up behind Fliss, pretending to be a ghost, and gave her the fright of her life. And that was how we got the idea.

"That's it, that's it," Kenny started to squeal. Then she lowered her voice. "Come on, let's go upstairs." We all scooted up to her room where she outlined her plan. It was ace. We were so excited we were hopping around the bedroom rubbing our hands.

Suddenly we heard the phone ring. It was Kenny's dad again. This definitely wasn't his day. Now his car had broken down. He'd already been to see his patient, but he was stuck and couldn't get home. Kenny's mum came into the bedroom looking really flustered.

"Listen, girls, I'm going to have to go and pick up Kenny's dad. Do you think you'll be OK with Emma and Hayley, while I'm gone?"

"Course we will," said Kenny. Emma often babysits for her and Molly.

"Well, I don't like leaving you all with Emma, and I wouldn't normally do it, but today hasn't exactly been a normal day. I won't be gone long."

"Don't worry about it," said Kenny. It was good news for us. Now we'd be able to creep in and scare Molly more easily, with both her parents out of the way. "Hang loose, Mother Goose," she said. "In fact, if you like we'll get ready for bed now."

That was a bit of a mistake because it made her mum suspicious. After all it was still only eight o'clock. "You're not going to make a lot of noise, are you, Laura, because Molly isn't very well and she's trying to rest."

"She looked all right to me," said Kenny. "She's faking, you know. It's just to get attention. You shouldn't give in to her."

Kenny's mum smiled and said, "Just try not to make too much noise and disturb her, all right?"

Kenny pulled a face, but nodded. It was perfect – her mum and dad would be out of the house; Emma and Hayley were busy downstairs in the kitchen; Molly was already in bed. We waited, as quiet as mice, in Kenny's room until we heard her mum's car start up and move off down the road.

"OK, let's get going," said Kenny.

"Who's going to do it?" I said. Everybody looked at me as if I'd asked a really stupid question. "Why me?"

"Because you're the biggest," said Kenny.

"So?"

"You look the most like a fully grown ghost," Rosie agreed.

"What's a fully grown ghost when it's at home?" I said.

"You know what she means," said Fliss.

I didn't, but there was no point arguing because I was outvoted, four to one. I wasn't sure it was such a good idea any more, but the others were all for it. It was

OK for them; they didn't have to do it.

I slipped the hairdressing gown over my head. Then Kenny poked about under her bed and found me a set of those long plastic finger nails. I put my hands under the gown and then Kenny fitted them onto the ends of my fingers. They looked really drastic.

The trouble started when we lifted the gown up to cover my face, I couldn't see a thing. As soon as I tried to move I walked into Kenny's bed.

"Ow! This is useless. I'll probably fall downstairs and break my neck," I yelled.

"Shhh!" said Kenny. "She'll hear you. Wait a minute. Take it off and I'll cut two eye holes in it."

Well, that was a real performance because the first time she cut them too close together and I still couldn't see a thing, so she had to cut a second set.

"Won't your mum hit the roof, when she sees what you've done?" said Fliss.

"She's got lots of these gowns. I'll get rid of this one. She'll never miss it."

At last we'd got two eye holes that I could just about see through. And then I had a little practice walking round the room in the dark. Kenny turned her light out and pulled back the curtains so a bit of light from the street lamps came through. The others said I looked dead creepy and I started to make sort of ghostly noises, until Fliss really started to freak.

"OK, that's enough practising," said Kenny. "Let's do it."

"Do what?" I said from under the cape. "What am I supposed to do?"

"Go in there and give her the scare of her life."

"What if I wake her up?"

"You'll have to wake her up or there's no point doing it," said Kenny.

"But what if she jumps out of bed and catches me?"

"As soon as she's awake you'll have to leg

it back to my room. Now, come on."

Kenny opened her bedroom door and listened. There was no sound from downstairs. The kitchen door was closed, so she pushed me forwards along the landing as far as Emma's bedroom door. It was closed too and I hadn't got a hand free, what with the gown and the finger nails, so Kenny bobbed in front of me, turned the door handle and opened the door. It made a loud creaking noise and I could hear Fliss gasp. I was ready to forget the whole thing too, but Kenny gave me another push and I ended up in the room.

It took ages for my eyes to get used to the dark and I walked into the end of the camp bed, trying to make out where Molly was. Fortunately she wasn't in it. She was in Emma's bed. I shuffled over to her and stood looking down on her and then I didn't know what to do next.

I knew the others were outside the room listening, so I thought about doing a few ghostly moans, but I was frightened of waking Molly up in case she caught me before I had a chance to scarper. Kenny had said just blow on her, but how could I do that with this rotten cape over my face. So, instead, I waved my hands about a bit to make a draught. I felt really stupid. And scared.

Suddenly something terrible happened. Molly's eyes opened and she stared right at me. I nearly died. I couldn't move. I was just glued to the spot. I felt as if I would never move again, until she screamed. I soon moved then.

She just screamed and screamed and screamed. It was deafening. I don't remember how I got along the landing. I ran straight into the others who were still crowding round outside the door. The next moment we'd fallen into Kenny's room, pushed the door shut and collapsed in a heap on Kenny's bed, stuffing our hands in our mouths so that we wouldn't give ourselves away.

"Quick, Frankie, quick," said Rosie. "Get that off."

It's a good job she said that because we'd just ripped the gown off and collected up the finger nails which shot all over the floor, and stuffed them under Kenny's pillow, when Emma and Hayley crashed into the room.

"Molly says someone just broke into her room. Are you all OK? Did you hear anything? You'd better come and help us look." Then they raced out again.

We all looked at each other and tried to arrange our faces so they didn't give us away and followed them out onto the landing. Molly was still screaming her head off.

CHAPTER EIGHT

"It's all right, Molly," said Emma, trying to calm her down. "You can stop making that terrible noise. It sounds as if you're being murdered."

"I could have been," she yelled.

"Kenny, are you sure you didn't hear anything?" Emma asked again.

"Not a thing," said Kenny. "We were just fooling about in my room. We didn't hear a sound, except for Monster-face screaming her head off."

"So would you if someone had been

standing over your bed. Have you looked? He might still be in the house."

We offered to search the house. We all ran up and downstairs like mad things, opening doors then banging them closed again. We raced into the kitchen and it was a good job we did because the chicken masala was burning so we yelled up to tell them and Hayley rushed down to turn it off.

Emma was still trying to calm Molly down and get some sense out of her but Molly wouldn't stop yelling, "I want my mum! I want my dad!" She was really enjoying herself. She was putting on a good act, but I could tell she wasn't really scared. I didn't like the way she kept looking at us. Somehow I was sure she knew it was me.

"Look," said Emma, "just stop shouting. Mum and Dad'll be home any time. They'll sort it out." You could tell she didn't know what to do for the best.

"It'll be too late by then," Molly insisted. "He'll have got away. You've got to ring the police."

"Don't be stupid," said Kenny. "We can't ring the police. Anyway, we've looked. There's no one here. You probably dreamt it."

"I didn't dream it. He was right here, standing over me. He was six feet tall and he had horrible claws. He'd probably have clawed my eyes out if I hadn't woken up."

"She just dreamt it," Kenny told Emma. "Or made it up. She's always making things up. You know what she's like."

Emma certainly knew what Molly was like, but she could see something funny was going on. And any minute now we could all see Kenny and Molly were going to get into one of their screaming matches, so Emma said, "Kenny go away and leave this to me. Take the others back to your bedroom. Now!"

"But she's just being stupid and making

it all up," Kenny started again.

"I am not," Molly screamed.

"Go! Now!" said Emma pointing to the door.

Kenny gave Molly a last nasty look and then we all trooped back to her bedroom. We didn't close the door because we wanted to try and hear what was going on. But Emma closed hers so, however much we strained our ears, we couldn't hear a sound.

We sat on Kenny's bedroom floor trying to enjoy our revenge.

"Did you see her face?" hissed Kenny.

"It was awesome," said Lyndz.

"She sounded like a banshee," said Rosie.

"He was six feet tall with horrible claws," I said, mimicking Molly's voice.

We were all giggling and hugging ourselves, but we couldn't really keep it up for long, because we couldn't help wondering what Molly was telling Emma.

"What do you think's going on?" said Fliss. She looked really scared. I couldn't see why because I was the one who was going to get into trouble if anybody did.

"Oh, don't worry about it," said Kenny. "Emma'll calm her down. She won't want mum to know there's been trouble or she won't get paid for looking after us."

Oh well, we thought, if Kenny isn't worried, there's no reason for the rest of us to be. But a couple of minutes later we had plenty to be worried about.

Emma came in and said she'd phoned the police and they were sending someone round straight away. I thought Kenny was going into orbit.

"What! Why! What do you mean? Police? You didn't need to ring the police."

"Well," said Emma, "Molly says there was definitely someone in her room so there must have been a prowler or something. Anyway, don't you worry, the police'll sort it out. They should be round any minute."

Kenny almost grabbed hold of Emma. "Mum and Dad'll go mad you know. You should have waited for them to come back. You know what Molly's like; she makes things up all the time. They'll be so mad when they find out."

But Emma stayed dead cool. "No, I'm sure they'd have done the same. Anyway you needn't worry about it," she said as she left the room. "Although," she turned and added, "they'll probably want a statement from each of you."

"A statement?" shrieked Fliss. "But I didn't see anything. It was nothing to do with me. It wasn't my idea. I didn't do anything."

That's just like Fliss when she gets in a flap. I could have murdered her. Kenny looked as if she could too.

"Nobody suggested *you'd* done anything, Fliss," said Emma, looking straight at me. "If you didn't hear a sound that's what you'll need to say to the inspector."

"Inspector!" said Kenny.

"Well, whoever they send," said Emma smiling. "I'm going to get on with my meal until they come."

After she went out we all sat there too shocked to speak. We were all white, in fact we looked like a gang of ghosts. Now we were in deep trouble.

"You're going to have to go and tell them the truth," said Fliss.

"No way," said Kenny.

"I think Molly knows anyway," I said. The others looked at me. "I've just got this feeling. I think she could tell it was me."

"What? So you mean she's putting it all on just to get us into trouble."

I nodded. "I think so."

"I still think you'd better tell Emma," said Fliss. "So she can ring the police and tell them not to come."

Lyndz nodded. "I agree with Fliss. Your

mum and dad'll go mad if they come home and find the police here."

"They're going to go mad anyway," said Kenny. "Emma's bound to tell them and I'll be grounded for the rest of my life, or longer. And just coming up for Christmas as well. I'll probably get no presents, no Christmas dinner, no TV for the whole week." We were all feeling sorry for Kenny, but we were feeling sorry for ourselves too.

"Oh, please, Kenny, go and tell Emma," Fliss begged her. "Before they come."

I couldn't decide what was best. I sort of agreed with Fliss. Better make a clean breast of it before her parents came back. And yet I knew how much Kenny would hate having to own up and let Molly think she'd won. But time was running out. They could be here any moment. We were just waiting for the doorbell to ring. Kenny sat there and wouldn't speak. She looked as if she'd turned to stone or something.

"I think we should vote on it," said Fliss. "Who thinks Kenny should go and tell Emma the truth?" She put her own hand straight up. Lyndz hesitated, then shrugged her shoulders and put her hand up too. Rosie slowly lifted hers. Kenny looked at each of them as if they were no friends of hers. Then she looked at me. My hand felt like a lump of lead.

Kenny was my best friend. We'd been friends since playschool. I didn't want to let her down but I could feel my hand starting to rise. Suddenly we heard a car coming along the road, slowing down and turning into their drive.

We all just about had heart attacks. Kenny jumped up off the bed, raced downstairs and burst into the kitchen. We were all just a step behind her.

"OK, it was us. We did it. It was just a joke. We didn't mean to scare her to death. It was..." Kenny stopped in mid sentence.

Emma and Hayley and Molly were sitting

at the breakfast bar eating chicken masala. They were all grinning like three fat cats that had got the cream. There was a heavenly smell of bananas cooking and I just kept thinking how we wouldn't get any now.

The truth dawned on Kenny and her face screwed up. She was just about to start screaming at them, when the front door opened and in walked her mum and dad.

"Are you girls still up and about?" said Kenny's mum. "I thought you'd have been in bed by now. Off you go and get ready and I'll bring you all a drink up." Then she spotted Molly. "Well, you're looking a bit brighter. I told you all you needed was a good rest."

"Mmm, mmm," said Kenny's dad. "Something smells good. Any left over?"

"You be careful," said her mum. "You've just had that tooth fixed. We don't want any more accidents. I'll make you some scrambled egg."

"Oh, thanks a lot. Baby food. Just what I need."

We all headed off upstairs thinking, well, at least we'd got away without being interviewed by the police, when we heard Monster-face say, "By the way, Dad. I found the rest of that cake in the bin. I think I know what you broke your tooth on."

We didn't hang around to hear any more. We went straight off to bed.

CHAPTER NINE

We all got into our sleeping bags, apart from Fliss and Kenny who had the beds. We turned on our torches and lay there whispering.

"What do you think they'll say in the morning?" I asked Kenny.

"Dunno." She sounded as if she didn't care much either. She was so mad with Molly, that was all she could think about.

It was bad enough that Molly had told Emma it was us and then got Emma to pretend she'd rung the police, and we'd fallen for it. But now she'd grassed on us to Kenny's dad about the spider in the cake. That was really the pits.

"It's just not fair," said Kenny. "How is it she always wins?"

"She doesn't always win," I said. "She might have realised afterwards that it was me, but when she first woke up she was really scared. You should have seen her face. She looked as if she was going to wet herself."

"Yeah," said Lyndz. "It was worth it. What does it matter if we get grounded again. They always tell us we're grounded forever, but they soon forget."

That's true, isn't it? Grown-ups haven't got very long memories.

"And it's been the best sleepover yet," said Rosie. "I'll never forget this one."

"Really?" said Kenny.

"Coo-el," I agreed.

"Anyway it's not over yet," said Fliss. "We've still got our midnight feast to have and our Christmas presents."

"Yeah, but that's another thing," said Kenny, miserably. "I still haven't got any of your presents. I hadn't got enough money and now I won't be able to get any more." She sounded as if she might start to cry, which I'd never seen Kenny do before.

"Look, it doesn't matter," said Lyndz. "I've only got little presents this year. I couldn't afford anything big like Fliss."

"Nor me," said Rosie. "I don't have much money."

Fliss looked a bit embarrassed. "Well, I didn't really have to pay for the tapes," she admitted. "Andy got them cheap from the man who owns the shop. He did some plastering for him. Anyway," she said, "it's like my mum says, it's not the gift that counts…"

We all joined in, "It's the thought behind it."

So I felt a lot better after that. We agreed that Kenny and I would give the others their presents on the last day at school. Rosie gave us each a cute pencil with the head of Pongo from *101 Dalmations* on it and a matching rubber.

But Lyndz's present was the best surprise. It was one big flat box wrapped in Christmas paper with a label which said: *To the Sleepover Club.*

We didn't know what to make of it.

"But who's going to open it?" said Fliss.

"All of us," said Lyndz. "I'll count. One… two… three…"

We all tore a bit of the paper until it was unwrapped. Inside was a box of five Christmas crackers. We could see through the cellophane there was one with each of our names on it. They looked dead good, really professional, but Lyndz and her mum had made them themselves.

Before we pulled them we sat round in a circle and instead of our usual Sleepover Club song, we sang, "Happy Christmas to us, Happy Christmas to us, Happy

Christmas, to the Sleepover Club, Happy Christmas to us." When we pulled the crackers they went off with a bang, like proper ones and they had a party hat inside and a joke and a present and a chocolate. I got a key ring with a little black cocker spaniel on it, just like my dog, Pepsi. It was brilliant.

We sat up wearing paper hats, reading out our jokes and eating our chocolates. Then we sang loads of Christmas carols. After that we had our midnight feast and it really was midnight; we heard the church clock chiming twelve.

When we snuggled down into our sleeping bags and turned off our torches, Kenny said, "I don't care what they say tomorrow, it was a good laugh, so it was worth it."

"It sure was," I said. "The best." And everyone agreed.

GOODBYE

Kenny's mum and dad had had plenty of time to calm down by the time we went home, so Kenny didn't really get into mega-trouble. She did get a good telling off about putting things in cakes, though, because it could have been dangerous. As her dad pointed out, someone could have choked on it which, to be honest, we hadn't really thought about.

Kenny wouldn't speak to Emma at first for taking Molly's side, even though Emma insisted she hadn't. She said she thought that after what we'd done to Molly we deserved a bit of a scare ourselves.

Molly was dead pleased with herself, and kept rubbing it in, so Kenny refused to speak to her for a whole week. But she couldn't keep it up because then it was Christmas and Molly did such a surprising thing. She got Kenny her very best Christmas present ever. It was an amazing pop-up book all about the body, with pictures of your insides and bits that move, with all the really gory bits. Kenny loved it. Molly had been saving for weeks and in the end she'd had to borrow a bit from their mum. So, you see, even gruesome older sisters can surprise you sometimes.

They had a truce which lasted for most of Christmas. It's over now, of course, because Molly trod on Kenny's picture of Emile Heskey and wouldn't apologise. He's a footballer who plays for Leicester City and Kenny worships him. But now he's got a big footprint right across his nose. So it's back to normal bedroom warfare at Kenny's.

But there you go. It was still a pretty good Christmas. My mum was dead pleased with her pig and I had a brain wave which meant I didn't need to spend lots of money on my friends. I remembered the photo Dad took of us the last time they sleptover at my house when we had the wedding! So I had copies made and put them in little plastic frames and everyone was really pleased because we all looked drop-dead gorgeous.

Which reminds me – everyone *lurved* my new shoes. They are really drastic. I'm trying to persuade Mum and Dad to let me wear them for school. They've said, "No way. Not a chance. Don't even ask." But they always say that at first. It might take a while, but don't worry, I'll get round them.

Anyway keep your fingers crossed for me. See you some time. Bye.

The Sleepover Club at Frankie's

Join the Sleepover Club: Frankie, Kenny, Felicity, Rosie and Lyndsey, five girls who just want to have fun – but who always end up in mischief.

Brown Owl's in a bad mood and the Sleepover Club are determined to cheer her up. Maybe she'd be happier if she had a new boyfriend. And where better than a sleepover at Frankie's to plan Operation Blind Date?

Pack up your sleepover kit and drop in on the fun!

0 00 675233 0

The Sleepover Club at Lyndsey's

Join the Sleepover Club: Frankie, Kenny, Felicity, Rosie and Lyndsey, five girls who just want to have fun – but who always end up in mischief.

The girls plan a great party for Lyndsey's birthday – fun, food, a spooky video and a sleepover. Definitely not for boys! But somehow Lyndsey's brothers make their presence felt and soon everyone's too scared to sleep.

Pack up your sleepover kit and drop in on the fun!

0 00 675234 9

The Sleepover Club at Felicity's

Join the Sleepover Club: Frankie, Kenny, Felicity, Rosie and Lyndsey, five girls who just want to have fun – but who always end up in mischief.

A sleepover isn't a sleepover without a midnight feast and when the food runs out and everyone's still hungry, the Sleepover Club tiptoe down to the kitchen. But – quick! – the toaster's on fire!

Pack up your sleepover kit and drop in on the fun!

0 00 675236 5